Luna Garza

ACCIDENTAL DETECTIVE

DREAM LAND

PJ GRAY

Luna Garza

ACCIDENTAL DETECTIVE

Bone Hills	Hindsight
Coal Spell	Main Stage
Dream Land	Scent of Blue
Found Glory	

SADDLEBACK
EDUCATIONAL PUBLISHING
www.sdlback.com

ISBN: 978-1-68021-994-4
eBook: 978-1-64598-849-6

Printed in Malaysia

26 25 24 23 22   1 2 3 4 5

For Carol

CHAPTER 1

DREAM TO NIGHTMARE

The teen girl fell into bed, humming to herself. She replayed the night in her head. Her party had been a huge success. It was a perfect summer night. All her friends had come. Best of all, her crush was there.

While dancing with a group of girls, she had locked eyes with him. He looked away. Feeling brave, she had gone over and pulled him into their dance party. Some boys had been lighting fireworks from her family's dock. As they danced, colors had exploded overhead. Her heart had felt like it was bursting too.

A warm summer breeze came through the open window. It made the curtains sway gently. The hour was late. Before long, the girl's eyes closed. She fell into a deep sleep.

When she woke up, her room was filled with smoke. The girl jumped out of bed and went to the window. It was still dark, but an eerie glow shone through the smoke.

"Oh no!" she gasped.

She ran downstairs. The smoke was so thick she could hardly breathe. In seconds, she was out the door and in the backyard.

Flames had engulfed the barn. They were licking the side of the house.

"No!" she shouted.

In her bare feet, she ran as fast as she could through the woods. Her nightgown got caught on a low tree branch, causing her to stumble. By the time she reached the neighbor's house, her feet were bloody.

When Mrs. Grant opened the door, half-asleep, she could see the flames dancing in the trees.

"Fire! Call 911!" the girl screamed. Then she collapsed on her neighbor's front porch, coughing uncontrollably.

CHAPTER 2

LAKE ARRIVAL

Luna Garza gazed out of the car window. It was a beautiful day for a drive. Amber Robbins, her best friend, was next to her in the back seat. Mrs. Garza was driving the girls to Lake Waman, where Amber's uncle lived.

"How far away is the lake?" Luna asked.

"About 20 miles outside of Apple Glen," Mrs. Garza answered. "Luna, can you please check the directions on your phone? I've never driven to the lake before, and I don't want us to get lost."

Luna rolled her eyes. "Come on, Mom. We

can't be lost. You've only been driving for ten minutes."

"I know," Luna's mom said. "But these winding roads are confusing."

"Don't worry, Mrs. Garza," Amber said. "I've been to the lake tons of times. This is the right way."

Luna smiled at her friend. Amber had grown up in Apple Glen and knew the area well. But Luna's family had moved to Ohio from California just a couple of years ago. At the time, Luna's parents were looking for a new adventure. They bought a big, old two-story house that needed a lot of work. The town of Apple Glen was similar in some ways. It had once been a bustling American town. Then it had fallen on hard times. People like the Garzas, however, had started moving in and trying to bring the town back to its former glory. While Mr. Garza traveled for his job, Mrs. Garza had worked on restoring their house. She learned so much that she eventually started her own business. Restoring furniture and objects for other people became her passion.

"I'm looking forward to meeting your uncle, Amber," Luna's mom said from the driver's seat. "His paintings are so beautiful."

"He's a painter?" Luna asked Amber. "You never told me that."

"Yes, and a well-known one too!" Mrs. Garza said. "I've seen some of his paintings of the lake at the gallery downtown."

"He does love to paint the lake," Amber said. Then she turned to Luna. "I can't believe you've never been there. We're going to have so much fun! This will be the best start to summer break ever."

When Amber had asked Luna if she wanted to spend a week at her uncle's house on the lake, Luna jumped at the chance. Mr. Robbins was going on a business trip, and Amber's mom had decided to join him. Amber's uncle was happy to have his niece visit. He'd even suggested she bring a friend. Luna was so happy her parents had let her go.

Amber leaned over to look out the windshield. "We're getting close," she said. "The house is up ahead." Then she pointed. "There it is on the right. See the red mailbox?"

The word *Boater* was painted in blue on the side of an old mailbox.

"Shouldn't it say *Robbins*?" Luna asked.

"Boater is my uncle's nickname."

Mrs. Garza carefully turned onto the long dirt driveway. It was lined with towering pine trees.

"Where's the lake?" Luna asked.

"It's close," Amber said. "You will see it once we get to the house."

A white two-story house with dark green shutters came into view. The front door was painted the same shade of forest green. Flower boxes hung under the windows. Colorful spring flowers spilled out of them.

As they got out of the car, Amber's uncle stepped onto the front porch to greet them. He was tall and slim with a short gray beard. His white pants and shirt were neatly pressed, and he wore a navy blue blazer. A straw hat with a white ribbon around it sat on his head. Luna thought he looked like a movie character.

"Welcome," he said to Mrs. Garza and Luna, shaking their hands. "I'm Rowland Robbins, but everyone calls me Boater." Then he winked at Amber. "Except Amber. I'm *Uncle* Boater to her."

Luna looked around at the house and the thick forest surrounding it. This would be home for a week. She took a deep breath. The fresh air smelled so nice. *What a perfect place to relax,* she thought.

CHAPTER 3

FLOWER POWER

After Luna said goodbye to her mom, Amber led Luna up to the guest room on the second floor. They unpacked their things and decided where they would sleep. Luna chose the bed next to the window.

Then they went downstairs to find Boater. As they passed the dining room, Amber noticed a large flower arrangement on the table.

"That's odd," she said, pointing at it and grinning. "Does my uncle have an admirer?" She and Luna giggled.

"Uncle?" Amber called out. "Where are you?"

They walked into the kitchen, where they found Boater preparing dinner.

"Hi, girls," he said. "Dinner will be ready shortly. Amber, why don't you show Luna around?"

Luna and Amber went out the back door to the patio. Just beyond the large sloping backyard was the lake. The late afternoon sun made the surface of the water sparkle. As they walked toward the shore, Luna noticed a small building on their left. It was painted like the main house. "What is that?" she asked.

"That's my uncle's studio," Amber said. "He paints there."

Luna looked around at the dense woods on either side of the property. "Does all of this land belong to your family?"

"Not all of it," Amber said. She pointed to the woods behind the art studio. "The land over there belongs to my family." Then she pointed to the other side of the backyard. "That land belongs to our neighbors, the Grants."

They walked past a fire pit with chairs around it. "Cool!" Luna said. "I love fire pits."

"Me too," Amber said. "We'll roast hot dogs one night."

Finally, they reached the lakeshore. There was a dock with a diving board at the end of it. A rowboat was tied to one side of the dock. On the other side, there was a small motorboat. Amber smiled. "This is where all of the fun happens."

Luna pulled out her phone. "It's beautiful here," she said, snapping a few pics. "Your uncle is so lucky to have this lake house."

"I know. See that one way over there?"

Amber pointed to a large house on the other side of the nearest cove. The sun was in Luna's eyes. She squinted to see it. "That's the Grant family's summer home. They'll probably be here soon. A path through the woods links our properties. I'll show you tomorrow."

"Wow," Luna said. "It looks like a mansion."

"Yeah. The place is a lot bigger than Uncle Boater's house. He said there used to be another house in between his and theirs. It's gone now. At some point the Grants bought the property. Then they tore their old house down and built that mansion."

Luna looked around. "I don't see any other houses."

"There are a few on the other side of the lake. It's hard to see them through the trees. Don't worry. We can be as loud as we want out here."

Luna laughed.

They heard Amber's uncle calling out from the back door. "Dinnertime!"

Amber and Luna made their way back to the house. In the dining room, the table was set with a platter of grilled chicken, bowls of roasted vegetables, and baked potatoes. The girls took their seats and began spooning food onto their plates.

Boater sat down at the head of the table and smiled. "Welcome to my home, Luna. I hope you enjoy it here at the lake."

"Thank you for having me," Luna replied. "This place is beautiful. Amber told me this house has been in your family for a long time. How old is it?"

"Zeb Robbins built the house in 1830. There were very few people in Apple Glen at that time."

"Was Zeb Robbins born here?" Luna asked.

"No. He grew up in New York. Then he traveled west as a young man. He wanted to study plants. In fact, Zeb wrote several books about native plants."

"Speaking of plants," Amber said quickly. "Where did *those* come from?" She pointed at the flower arrangement, which Boater had moved to a side table.

Luna hid a smile with her napkin.

Boater sat up in his chair. "Why do you ask?"

"Well," Amber said, her cheeks flushing. "We wondered if you might have an admirer."

He laughed. "Oh, my dears. You have the wrong idea. Those flowers are from a real estate agent. Her name is Markie Lasser."

"Is she fond of you?" Luna asked.

"Good heavens, no. She is fond of this house and property. Markie and I knew each other growing up. For years, she has been asking if

I want to sell this house. Her idea is to turn it into a bed and breakfast." He looked down and continued to cut his piece of chicken. "Let's talk about more interesting subjects. Luna, your mother mentioned the summer project you girls are doing. Tell me about it."

"Apple Glen is hosting a summer program for middle school students," Luna said. "It's called City Clean and Green. We're helping to clean up the city and spread the word about green technology."

"Many of our classmates have joined," Amber added. "Luna and I are going to be in charge of a group in the downtown area."

"That's great," Boater said. "Your mother explained that you'll need a ride to the city a few times a week. I usually don't go into town that often. But this program sounds very beneficial to the city, and I'm happy to support you in it."

He raised his glass of iced tea. Amber and Luna raised theirs too. "May your visit here be memorable," he said.

Luna and Amber grinned at each other as they clinked their glasses.

CHAPTER 4

NIGHT VISION

After dinner, Boater lit a fire in the pit outside. They sat around it and roasted marshmallows.

"Boater, may I ask how you got your nickname?" Luna said as she carefully rotated her marshmallow in the fire.

"Of course," Boater replied. "My birth name is Rowland. In school, I was on the rowing team. Because of that and my name, friends called me Row. My mother did not care for that name, so she started calling me Boater. It wasn't long before the name caught on."

Amber looked surprised. "Wow. I never knew that."

Her uncle chuckled and turned to Luna. "I like your name, Luna. Do you know why your parents chose it for you?"

"It's not that exciting. I was born during a full moon."

Boater looked up. "The moon is almost full tonight. Tomorrow night it should be completely full."

The three chatted for a while longer. Luna and Amber stuffed themselves with marshmallows. Eventually the fire died down, and they all began to yawn. "We should turn in," Boater announced. "You girls have a big day tomorrow."

Amber and Luna went upstairs and got ready for bed. Luna was glad to be sleeping near the window. The warm summer breeze coming through it felt good. Before long, she was asleep.

Hours later, a sound outside woke Luna. She rolled over in her bed. *What's that?* she wondered. It sounded like a horse whinnying.

Luna sat up and looked at Amber across the room. Her friend was still asleep.

The whinnying turned to a squeal. It made the hair on Luna's arms stand up. She pulled a pillow over her head and tried to go back to sleep. But the noise did not stop.

Luna was wide awake now. She looked out the window. All she could see were tree branches in the moonlight. *I don't remember seeing any stables,* she thought. *Does Boater have a horse? Why would it make that noise?*

Luna got out of bed and carefully tiptoed out of the room. She went downstairs and into the kitchen. Slowly, she opened the back door. The whinnying and squealing continued. It seemed to be coming from the woods behind the art studio.

The moonlight cast shadows through

the trees. Luna crept into the yard, walking toward the noise. For some reason, she did not feel scared. All she could think about was that an animal might be hurt and need help.

Suddenly, a rustling noise came from some bushes beside the art studio. Luna walked around them. Her eyes took in a strange sight in the darkness. She gasped.

There was a large, fawn-colored horse lying on the grass behind the bushes. It appeared to be struggling to breathe. The whinnying noise came with each labored exhale.

A strange scent entered Luna's nose. She had smelled it before when she accidentally held the curling iron on her hair too long. It was the odor of burning hair and skin.

Luna was not sure whether it was safe to get any closer to the horse. The animal was clearly in trouble.

Realizing she needed to get help, Luna ran back through the dark yard. Her mind was racing. *Where did the horse come from? What happened to it? Is it Boater's horse? Why hadn't he or Amber mentioned it earlier?*

CHAPTER 5

VANISHED

Luna reached the back door of the house and threw it open. She sprinted through the dark kitchen, up the stairs, and into the guest room.

"Amber!" she said in a loud whisper, shaking her friend awake. "Wake up!"

"Huh?" Amber sat up, startled. "Is there a fire? What's happening?"

"We need to call 911. No, wait—we need a veterinarian!"

"A vet?" Amber turned on the lamp beside her bed. "Why?"

"There's a horse out by your uncle's studio. It's badly hurt."

Amber stared at Luna for a moment. "You're joking, right?"

"No. This isn't a joke."

"Then you must have had a bad dream." Amber shook her head. "Maybe you ate too many marshmallows."

"Amber, we need to tell your uncle. A horse is dying out there. We have to get help!"

"Okay, wait a second." Amber spoke slowly. "Let's take a deep breath. First, I don't think we should wake up my uncle yet." She stepped out of her bed. "I'll grab a flashlight. Then you can show me what you saw."

"Don't you believe me?" Luna asked.

Amber glanced at a clock on the nightstand. "Well, Luna, it's after midnight. I believe you. But I'm also not sure you were fully awake when you saw the horse."

Quietly, Luna hurried Amber out of the house. She took the flashlight and led the way toward the studio. When they reached the grass, Luna broke into a run across the yard. "Wait!" Amber said. "Slow down!"

The woods hummed with the sounds of frogs and crickets. Luna could no longer hear the horse.

"Do you even know where you're going?" Amber asked, trying to keep up.

"Shhh!" Luna replied.

"Why are we whispering?"

"The horse is injured. We don't want to scare it."

Luna stopped at the bushes where she had seen the horse. "It's behind here." She took a few careful steps closer and then shined the light behind the bushes. But the horse wasn't there.

"Wait," Luna said. "Where did it go?"

"Are you sure this is where you saw it?"

"Yes." Luna looked around frantically. "I'm positive."

"What *exactly* did you see?"

"There was a horse! It was lying on the ground behind these bushes. The poor thing was clearly in pain."

Amber stared at Luna expressionless for a moment. Then she grabbed the flashlight out of Luna's hand and shined it through the trees. "There's nothing out here, Luna. My uncle doesn't have a horse. Neither do the Grants."

"It doesn't make sense," Luna said slowly. "I know what I saw."

Amber turned around and marched back toward the house. Luna followed.

"Amber, I'm sorry, but—"

"Luna, you had a dream." Amber sounded exasperated. "Forget about it. Just chalk it up to seeing ghosts or spirits or whatever it is that seems to happen to you everywhere you go."

"But can we at least wake up your uncle and—"

Amber suddenly stopped and turned. She pointed the light at Luna's face. "No. We aren't going to tell my uncle about this. He doesn't need to know about the imaginary dying horse in his backyard! Do you want to be able to come here again?"

Luna looked down. Amber had never been so cross with her before.

They walked back into the house in silence.

Luna could not go back to sleep. She listened for the horse all night but did not hear it again.

CHAPTER 6

NOT SO GOOD MORNING

The next morning, Amber got up and dressed without speaking to Luna. She brushed her hair silently while staring into the bedroom mirror.

Luna finally broke the silence. "I'm sorry about last night."

Amber turned and smiled at her. "I'm sorry too. I shouldn't have gotten so upset. Perhaps you were sleepwalking."

Luna shook her head. "No, I wasn't. The horse was real. I'm sure it was."

Amber changed the subject. "Come on.

Let's go downstairs. My uncle is set in his ways. He'll be mad if we're late for breakfast."

Boater greeted them in the kitchen. On the counter, there was a platter loaded with pancakes. Luna and Amber helped themselves and sat down at the kitchen table.

"Did you sleep well?" Boater asked. He passed Amber the pitcher of orange juice.

Amber glanced at Luna. "I slept okay."

Luna felt guilty and could not hold back. "No, we didn't sleep well. It was my fault."

Amber kicked Luna's leg under the table.

"Your fault?" Boater asked, sipping his coffee.

"I woke Amber up and made her go outside last night."

"Luna, stop," Amber whispered.

Boater looked confused. "Outside?"

"Yes," Luna went on. "There was a noise outside in the middle of the night. It sounded like a horse. So I went in the backyard to look around. I found an injured horse behind the bushes next to the studio. Then I ran back to the house and woke up Amber."

Boater looked serious. "An injured horse?"

"It was nothing," Amber said quickly.

"Yes, the horse was lying down and couldn't seem to get up," Luna said.

Boater looked at Amber. "Why didn't you wake me?" he asked.

Amber was quiet. Then she looked at her uncle. "I didn't see the horse. Only Luna did. When she took me out there, it was gone."

"That's odd," Boater said. "I don't know anyone in the area who has horses now. Several neighbors had them when I was growing up. Are you sure it was a horse, Luna?"

"Yes." Luna felt foolish. "Maybe it was wild."

"Perhaps," Boater said, rubbing his chin. "The Grants just returned to their house for the summer. I'll ask them if they have seen anything unusual." Boater looked at his watch. "You two should get your things. We need to leave soon or you'll be late."

Amber and Luna grabbed their backpacks and then got into Boater's car. The ride to the community center in downtown Apple Glen was quiet. There was no more talk of the horse in the woods.

Luna's eyes felt heavy from the night of poor sleep. She struggled to keep them open. It was the first day of the City Clean and Green summer program, and she needed to stay awake. She and Amber were going to lead a team of students. Faculty members from Apple Glen Middle School would be there. Members of the mayor's office were helping too.

When they finally reached the community center, Amber and Luna stepped out of the car. Luna immediately saw their classmate

Buddy Cross near the door. He liked to give Luna and Amber a hard time.

"Oh no," Luna groaned. "Buddy's here. Why? I thought he said that he would never join this group."

"Great," Amber said sarcastically. "Just what we need."

CHAPTER 7

INTRODUCTIONS

The first day of the City Clean and Green program was both an orientation and a chance for students to get organized. Luna and Amber already knew they would be leading a team. What they didn't know was who would be on it.

After a welcome presentation, their principal told everyone they'd be getting assigned to teams. Each team would have its own set of tasks to focus on.

As the principal started assigning people to Luna and Amber's group, they looked at each other. Both of them knew what the other was thinking. *Not Buddy Cross.*

There was only one name left to be called for their team. Luna and Amber held their breath.

"And last but not least, Buddy Cross," the principal said. Then he looked at Amber and Luna. "Your group will be collecting signatures for new solar-powered trash cans to be used downtown. You'll also be picking up litter in the park."

Buddy snickered as he walked over to join their group. Then he sat with his arms crossed. Luna tried not to look at him. She and Amber talked to the team about their job. Soon parents began to arrive. It was time for the meeting to end.

After most of the other kids left, Luna and Amber approached Buddy.

"Why are you here?" Luna asked him. "You clearly don't want to help."

"I have no choice," Buddy said. "My stepmom forced me."

A blonde woman in a plum-colored business suit walked up to them. Her long nails were painted silver. "There you are, Buddy. I've been looking for you." She smiled at Luna and Amber, revealing perfectly straight, white teeth. "Buddy? Aren't you going to introduce me to your friends?"

"Friends?" he replied. "Do you mean them?"

The girls ignored him. "Hi, I'm Luna Garza. You must be Buddy's mom."

"Stepmom," Buddy said quickly.

The woman glared at Buddy. Then she smiled again as she shook Luna's and Amber's hands. "Hi. I'm Markie Lasser. Pleasure to meet you."

Luna suddenly remembered the flowers in Boater's dining room. "Oh! *You're* Markie Lasser!" she exclaimed.

Markie smiled. "You must recognize me from my ads around the city. I buy and sell real estate."

Amber gave Luna a look. Then she introduced herself without using her last name. She did not want Markie to ask about her uncle. "We've seen your picture on the bus stop benches," Amber said politely.

"Can we go now?" Buddy interrupted. "You promised to buy me lunch."

"All right, all right," Markie sighed. "Hold your horses." She turned back to Luna and Amber. "I just wanted to say that I think this program is wonderful. And I'm so impressed with all of you. Keep up the good work. And let me know if I can help in any way."

Amber nodded. "Thank you very much!"

Luna watched Buddy and his stepmom walk away. "Wow," she said. "So that's Markie Lasser. She seems nice. How can she stand living with Buddy Cross? I feel sorry for her."

"I do too," Amber said. "Buddy isn't her only problem. Uncle Boater will never sell his house. There aren't enough flowers in the world to change his mind."

CHAPTER 8

MAGICAL PLACE

There was no meeting for the City Clean and Green program the next day. Amber and Luna were excited to have the whole day to themselves. After breakfast, they went down to the lake to swim. The water was still cool but the sun was shining. They practiced their diving skills. When they were tired of swimming, they took out the rowboat.

Back at the dock, the girls could hear music.

"Uncle Boater must be in his studio," Amber explained. "He likes to turn up the music while he paints."

They went into the house for lunch. As they ate, Luna's mind wandered back to the injured horse. She hadn't said anything else about it after breakfast the previous day. But she was still convinced it hadn't been a dream. *What if the animal is still out there?* she wondered.

"Let's go for a walk in the woods after lunch," Amber said. It was as if she had read Luna's mind.

"Sounds great." Luna smiled.

"Maybe we'll find some cool bugs," Amber said. "I'll show you the path to the Grant family's house too."

Their walk had just begun when Amber's phone buzzed.

"It's a text from my uncle," she said, looking at her phone. "He says to come back to the house."

"Why?" Luna asked. She tried not to let

Amber see her disappointment at the walk being cut short.

"Remember how I told you my uncle is kind of a foodie?" Amber grinned. "He wants to give us a cooking lesson."

"What? I don't know how to cook."

"Me neither. I think that's why we're getting a lesson."

The girls spent the rest of the afternoon in the kitchen. Boater taught them how to make potato salad. "We'll have this with our hot dogs tonight," he said.

"Yes! Roasting hot dogs is my favorite!" Amber said. She gave Luna a high five.

Soon it was time for dinner. Amber helped Boater carry a table from the patio to the dock. Luna carried the patio chairs. As the sun began to set over the lake, Boater lit a fire in the pit. They roasted hot dogs and sang campfire songs. Luna took pictures to send to her mom and dad. She didn't want the day to end. The lake felt like a magical place.

Later, Luna lay in bed thinking about the day. A warm, gentle breeze blew through the window. She closed her eyes. But something kept her awake. It was a crunching sound. Luna tried to ignore it. Then it grew louder.

"Amber?" Luna whispered. There was no response. She got up and tiptoed over to Amber's bed.

When she got closer to her friend, Luna figured out where the sound was coming from. Amber was grinding her teeth as she slept.

Luna rolled her eyes. Then she tried to wake Amber.

"Hey," she whispered. "Wake up. You're grinding your teeth."

Amber didn't move. She was in a deep sleep. Luna went back to her bed and sat on the edge. *Now what am I going to do?* she thought. *It's past midnight and I'm wide awake.*

Then she had an idea. She stood up and grabbed the flashlight Amber had found. Luna had to know the truth about the horse in the woods.

CHAPTER 9

THE SHED

Luna walked out into the backyard. The sky was clear, and the moon shone almost as brightly as the night before. Carefully, Luna approached the bushes next to the studio, shining her flashlight all around. She listened for the whinnying sound. But Luna only heard frogs croaking and insects buzzing.

She took a few steps past the bushes and aimed her light into the woods. Suddenly, something caught her eye. A shadow moved between the trees.

Holding her breath, Luna walked slowly toward the shadow. Pine needles crunched beneath her feet. A twig cracked. The shadow darted into what appeared to be a pile of wood.

As Luna got closer, she could see that it wasn't a pile of wood at all. It was a broken old shed covered in vines. Part of the roof was missing. Boards from the walls were too. The whole thing leaned to the left at a steep angle.

Luna aimed her light into the structure. She saw something move inside. Then she heard whimpering. Her heart began to race. It couldn't be the horse. The shed was too small for a horse to fit inside. *Is it a wild animal?* she wondered.

Holding her breath, Luna crept close enough to get a good view inside the shed. What she saw was not a wild animal. It was a yellow dog.

Luna knelt down. "Hi, pup," she said softly. "What are you doing out here?"

The dog let out a pitiful whine.

"Where did you come from?" Luna asked. "Don't worry. I won't hurt you. Do you want to come with me? Maybe I can help you get back home."

The dog continued to cower in the corner of the shed.

"Are you hungry?" Luna asked. "Come with me. I'll take you to the house. We'll get you some food. Then we can find out where you live." When Luna stepped closer, the dog backed against the wall. It looked more frightened than before. Then it turned around.

Luna gasped. There was no hair on the dog's tail and backside. Its skin looked red and blistered.

"What happened to you?" Luna whispered. "You're hurt. It's okay. Just stay there. I'll come back with help." She began to walk quickly back toward the house. Then she turned around to see if the dog might follow. Her flashlight lit up the old wooden structure.

The yellow dog was gone.

Luna's mind filled with questions as she walked back to the house. *How did the dog vanish so quickly? Where did it go? What had happened to it? Was it even real?*

CHAPTER 10

AN OLD DOG

The next morning was chaotic. It felt like a school day to Luna. Everyone woke up late. Boater made the girls fruit smoothies for breakfast so they could drink them in the car. Before they knew it, they were on the road to downtown Apple Glen.

"Sorry," Boater said as he drove. "I usually like to sit down for breakfast."

"That's okay," Amber said from the back seat. "The smoothies are great! And we'll be on time for our meeting."

Luna sat in the front seat and stared out of the car window. It was the first chance she had to think about the night before. *Was the dog real?* she wondered. *Or was it like the horse? Why am I seeing injured animals in the woods?*

Luna turned to see Amber staring down at her phone. She decided it was a good time to find out what Boater might know.

"Do any of your neighbors have dogs?" Luna asked.

"Dogs?" Boater looked confused.

"I . . . thought I heard one barking last night. Just wondered where it was coming from."

"Hmm." Boater furrowed his brow. "No, I don't believe anyone nearby has a dog. Perhaps you heard a coyote. We see them around sometimes."

"Oh, that's neat." Luna smiled. "This definitely sounded like a dog though."

"None of the neighbors have had dogs for

years," Boater went on. Then he paused. Luna sensed he wanted to say more. She waited.

"When I was growing up, the Lasser family had a dog," he said finally. "It was a yellow Lab. That dog loved to swim in the lake." Boater had a faraway look in his eyes.

"The Lasser family?" Luna asked. "You mean Markie Lasser, the real estate lady? Did she live at the lake too?"

Boater nodded. "Markie's family owned the property next door. But they sold it to the Grants when Markie and I were in high school. Seems like ancient history now!"

Luna realized that the car had stopped. They had arrived at the community center. She turned to Boater, hoping to ask him more questions.

Amber had already opened her door. "Come on, Luna!" she said. "We're going to be late."

CHAPTER 11

STRANGE ENCOUNTER

It was hard for Luna to concentrate during their morning meeting. Amber could tell something was wrong. But Luna was not ready to talk about what she had seen in the woods. None of it made sense to her, and she didn't want Amber to get angry with her again.

After the meeting ended, they started on their tasks. Amber led half of their group on litter patrol. Luna took the other half to gather signatures from community members who supported getting solar-powered trash cans for downtown.

As Luna's group walked through the downtown area, she spotted Markie Lasser. Buddy's stepmom was leaving a restaurant. A man dressed in a nice suit was with her. Luna remembered that Markie had offered to help them. She thought this would be a good time to approach her. If she could get a meeting with Markie Lasser, maybe she could find out more about her family's yellow Lab too.

"Ms. Lasser!" Luna called, waving.

Markie seemed caught off guard as she turned to Luna. "Well, hello . . . Luna, right?"

"Yes." Luna smiled. "I'm sorry to interrupt. We were just wondering if you might sign our petition. It supports the city's purchase of solar-powered trash cans for downtown."

"Oh, of course," Markie said. She took the clipboard Luna was holding out to her. Luna turned to the man in the suit.

"Sir, would you like to sign too?" she asked. "We need all the signatures we can get."

Markie gave her companion a forced smile. "Luna, this is Mr. John Price," she said. "He's here visiting from Columbus. Mr. Price works for Congressman Larry Firt."

Mr. Price shook Luna's hand.

Markie continued. "Luna goes to school with my stepson, Buddy. She's a very active citizen of Apple Glen, as you can see."

Luna blushed. "Thank you, Ms. Lasser. I could say the same of you. That's another reason I stopped you. Are you still interested in helping our city cleanup program? My friend Amber Robbins and I are in charge of a team and would love to meet with you."

"Wait," Mr. Price said with a smile. "Did you say Amber Robbins? Is she related to Boater Robbins?"

Markie Lasser's face fell suddenly. "Just

look at the time," she said, grabbing Mr. Price's arm. "We really should be going."

"Could we schedule a meeting?" Luna asked quickly.

Markie pulled a set of keys out of her purse and pushed a button. A black car next to them started instantly. She reached for the door handle as she looked at Luna. "Yes, yes," she said. "Stop by my office anytime. We'll talk."

Luna watched the car pull out of the parking spot and drive off.

"That was weird," she said under her breath.

CHAPTER 12

ODD ONE OUT

The next morning, Amber and Luna stood on the edge of the dock. Amber held out her phone for a selfie. "Smile!" she said. Then she snapped the pic. Luna giggled as she immediately turned around and jumped off the dock into the lake.

"Wait for me!" Amber shouted. "I want to post this." She quickly typed "Loving the lake with my bestie!" and then added three heart emojis to her caption.

It was another beautiful summer day on the lake. The girls had the day off from their program in the city. Uncle Boater was painting in his studio.

"What is he listening to?" Luna asked as she climbed back onto the dock. Music was wafting out from the studio again.

"I think it's jazz," Amber said. "He likes it loud."

Luna listened to the rhythm. She wanted to ask Boater more questions about the Lassers' dog and the shed in the woods, but he had been painting all day.

Then she had an idea.

"I'm going to the house to get a drink," she said to Amber. "Do you want one?"

"Sure! Bring me some water, please."

Luna walked up the sloping backyard toward the house. The studio door was open, and she could see Boater painting inside as she passed.

In the house, Luna opened the fridge and

grabbed three bottles of water. As she was walking out the back door, she heard the crunch of gravel on the driveway.

Is Boater expecting a visitor? she thought.

Luna turned around and walked through the house to the large front window. She saw a black car slowly coming up the driveway. Then it stopped. The car was too far away to see who was in it. After a few moments, it reversed down the driveway away from the house.

They must be lost, Luna thought.

She walked back through the kitchen and headed outside with the bottles of water. Boater's music was still playing loudly as she approached the studio. Through the open door, she could see him rinsing paintbrushes in a sink. *How can I get his attention?* Luna wondered.

She stood by the door and waved her arms

while still holding the bottles of water. Finally, Boater saw her and smiled. He turned the stereo volume down.

"Sorry about that," he said. "The music helps me channel my muse."

Luna handed him a bottle of water. "I thought you might like one of these," she said, looking past Boater into the studio. "This is a cool space."

"Thanks! Would you like to check it out?"

Luna nodded and walked inside. The studio was large and open. A half-finished painting stood on an easel in the middle of the room. There was a stack of blank canvases in one corner. Windows lined the walls near the ceiling.

"The windows are up so high," Luna said.

"Yes, it gives me space to hang my art on the walls," Boater said. "The windows aren't in the way. And there's lots of natural light. That's very important when painting."

Luna scanned Boater's paintings on the walls. Many were lake scenes, with lots of blue and green. One painting stood out from the rest. The canvas popped with red, orange, and yellow.

"Can I take a closer look at that one?" Luna asked, pointing to it.

For a moment, Boater seemed to hesitate. Then, with a polite smile, he said, "Of course!"

Luna walked over to the painting. It showed a barn on fire. Bright flames leapt from the structure. There were dark shadows in the forest background. Gray and white smoke mixed with the deep blue night sky.

"Wow," Luna said. "This painting is so realistic. May I ask what inspired it?"

"Oh, nothing in particular," Boater said nonchalantly. He took a sip of water. "Did I mention this building is an old barn? For a while, my family used it as a shed. I eventually cleaned it up to make this art studio."

The word *shed* made Luna think about the injured dog she had seen in the woods.

"Speaking of sheds," Luna said carefully. "I thought I saw a very old shed in the woods. Did that belong to your family too?"

Boater shook his head. "I don't recall another shed." Then he became more serious. "Listen, I don't want you and Amber going too far into the woods alone. There are bears and other wild animals out there. My grandfather used to set traps to catch them. Some of those traps could still be out there too."

Amber quietly poked her head into the doorway. "Boo!" she yelled.

Luna jumped. Amber and her uncle laughed.

"Where have you been?" Amber said to Luna. "I'm dying of thirst!"

CHAPTER 13

EAVESDROPPING

The next day, the community center was buzzing. Members of Luna and Amber's group were chatting excitedly in a circle. They held large empty garbage bags in their hands. Amber was passing out bright green baseball caps to everyone.

"May I have your attention?" Luna shouted over the group. They hushed and turned to look at her. "Do you all know your assignments?" The students nodded. "Great. We'll walk downtown together. Then each team will pick up litter on their assigned streets. Make sure you wear your caps. The police department knows what we're doing today. They will be watching out for us. Stay with your team leader. Call or text me or Amber if you have any problems. Everyone will meet back here this afternoon."

"Ready?" Amber asked with a big smile. "Let's go!"

The students marched out of the building and separated into their teams. Amber approached Luna.

"What time is your meeting with Buddy's stepmom?" she asked.

"I didn't make an appointment," Luna said. "She told me to stop by anytime. So I'm heading there first. Then I'll meet you to pick up trash. It shouldn't take long. By the way, where *is* Buddy?"

Amber rolled her eyes. "Did you really expect him to show up for this?"

"I should have known better." Luna

sighed. "See you later. Text me where you are so I can find you."

Luna walked several blocks to Markie Lasser's real estate office. She had told Amber that she was going to ask for Markie's help with getting donations from local businesses. These would be used to pay for the solar-powered trash cans. But Luna hoped she could also find out more about the Lasser family's lake house and the dog Boater had mentioned.

When she arrived at Markie's office, Luna entered the small front lobby. There was nobody at the reception desk. A door on the other side of the room had a gold plate with Markie's name on it. Luna went to the door and noticed that it was open a crack. She could hear Markie on the phone.

"Yes, I understand," Markie said. There was a pause. "Don't worry, Congressman. You'll get your resort. I can make it happen."

Luna leaned in closer. She could hear the

congressman talking loudly through Markie's phone.

"Markie," he said angrily. "I don't think you understand. We are about to lose the chance at *millions of dollars*. Make the deal. It doesn't matter how. Just get it done. Time is running out. This developer won't wait forever. Call me as soon as it's done."

"Will do, Larry," Markie replied. Her tone was short. Then she hung up the phone. As soon as she did, it rang again.

"Hi," Markie answered. "Yes, I just got off a call with him. It's time to get this done one way or another. I want my money too. You know how sick I am of Ohio. This will finally be my ticket out of here!"

She wants to leave Ohio? Luna was surprised. Markie had seemed so invested in the community.

It was clear to Luna that this wasn't a

good time to approach Markie about helping their program or anything else. She turned and quietly left the office.

As she walked to the park, a thought occurred to Luna. Boater had told them Markie wanted to buy his house. She planned to open a bed and breakfast by the lake. But Markie just said she couldn't wait to get out of Ohio. *Something doesn't add up*, Luna thought.

Her phone buzzed in her pocket. It was a text from Amber. "I'm near Elm Street, turning west."

CHAPTER 14

WHERE THERE'S SMOKE

Even though the day had been busy, Luna still had trouble falling asleep that night. She lay in bed listening to Amber grind her teeth. There was too much on her mind. The phone call she overheard in Markie's office made her wonder what Markie and the congressman were up to. *Why would Markie act like she was interested in buying Boater's house if she was planning to leave the state?*

Luna also felt unsettled about the animals she had seen in the forest. They seemed so real to her. *Could they really have just been dreams?* Boater had mentioned that the

Lassers had a yellow Lab. That was the same kind of dog Luna had seen in the shed. But there was no way that dog could still be alive.

Luna tossed and turned. Part of her wanted to go search the woods again. But Boater's warning made her hesitant. Finally, she fell asleep.

A strange crackling noise woke Luna. She bolted up in bed and looked at the clock on the nightstand. It read 2:37.

What is that? she wondered, rubbing her eyes. She peered out the window. The sky was pitch-black. That's when Luna smelled smoke. *Is someone having a bonfire?*

Luna looked over at Amber. Her friend was still sound asleep. Slowly, Luna got out of bed and grabbed the flashlight. Then she carefully padded down the stairs and into the kitchen.

The house was dark. Luna went to the back door and looked out. Even though it was the middle of the night, she half-expected to see Boater sitting by the bonfire. But what she actually saw was far more shocking. There was an eerie orange glow in the forest to her right. Smoke was rising, blocking out the moon and stars.

"Fire!" Luna gasped.

Without thinking, she opened the back door and ran into the yard. From there, she could see red and orange flames licking the trees. They were still several hundred yards away.

I need to call for help, Luna thought. Just as she turned to run inside, she heard another strange noise. A rhythmic clomping grew louder and louder. As she looked back toward the forest, a horse burst through the trees, flames dancing on its tail.

Before Luna could even process what she saw, the horse disappeared into the forest behind Boater's studio.

"Help! Fire!" Luna screamed as she ran back into the house.

The next thing she knew, Amber's face was staring down at her. Luna was in bed.

"Wake up," Amber whispered. "You're having a nightmare."

CHAPTER 15

RING A BELL

Ding! Ding! Ding!

A bell woke Luna up. Sunlight was flooding the bedroom. She rolled onto her back and rubbed her eyes. *Am I still dreaming?*

Ding! Ding! Ding!

The ringing seemed to be coming from the kitchen. *Is there a fire?* Luna wondered. She hopped out of bed, threw on her robe, and raced downstairs.

"Good morning, sleepyhead," Boater said, smiling. He was standing at the counter.

Luna looked around. "I heard a bell. It sounded like the kind at the fire station."

Boater pointed to a brass bell mounted on the wall. "Sometimes I ring that to wake up sleepy guests," he said with a wink. "Sit down and have some juice. Breakfast is almost ready."

"Sorry. I didn't mean to sleep so late. Why didn't Amber wake me?" Then Luna realized her friend wasn't there. "Where is Amber?"

Boater laughed. "We're out of bread. She took my bike and went to the small store up the road."

Luna yawned and took another sip of juice.

"Did you not sleep well last night?" he asked. Then he cracked an egg into a mixing bowl.

"I had a bad dream," Luna said. She paused. "It was about a fire. In the woods. Kind of like your painting."

"Ah," Boater replied. "Art can be suggestive. It can grab hold of the subconscious. That's one of the reasons I love it."

Luna nodded slowly.

"There was something else," she said. "I saw a horse again. This time, it ran through the yard. Its tail was on fire."

"Wow," Boater said somberly. "You know, Amber told me that you are a creative soul. You have an active imagination too. I know that can be troubling sometimes."

"It's strange," Luna went on. "In the past, I've had . . . spirits communicate with me. This feels like one of those times. Do you know if a fire ever happened in these woods?"

Luna waited for Boater to answer. He continued scrambling the eggs. After a few moments, he looked at Luna. "That doesn't ring a bell."

It was clear to Luna that if Boater knew something, he was not going to share it with her. But there was one person she knew who could always help her find answers about the past. Perhaps it was time to visit Joyce, her favorite librarian at the Apple Glen Public Library.

Just then, the kitchen door swung open. Amber stood there holding a loaf of bread. "I'm back!" She smiled at Luna. "Good morning. Did he ring that awful bell to wake you up?" Luna rolled her eyes and nodded.

"Hey!" Boater said, pretending to be offended. "Leave my bell alone."

CHAPTER 16

BINGO

After breakfast, Uncle Boater drove them to the community center again. It was the last day of the City Clean and Green program. There would be a party in the afternoon. Parents were invited too.

Inside the center, the mood was light. Everyone was excited about the party, but Luna's mind was elsewhere. She had to figure out a way to get to the library. During the morning meeting, Amber took charge. First she assigned team members to help decorate for the party. Then she checked her clipboard.

"Hanson's Bakery donated a cake," she said. "But someone will have to pick it up."

The bakery is right next to the library! Luna thought. Her hand shot into the air. "Me!" she said loudly. "I'll pick up the cake!"

Amber laughed. "Okay. Thanks, Luna."

"I'll be right back," Luna said as she turned to leave.

"Wait!" Amber replied. "You don't need to go right now, do you?"

Luna thought fast. "Sure I do. We don't want anything to happen to that cake. Don't worry. I'll be right back." She ran to the door.

"Do you need help?" Amber called to her. "It might be a big cake."

"No, thanks! I'll be fine. See you later!"

Luna ran several blocks through downtown Apple Glen until she reached the library. Once inside, she was happy to see Joyce standing behind the counter. Luna explained what she was looking for.

"Fires near the lake?" Joyce asked.

"Yes," Luna replied. "I've been staying with my friend out there. We wondered if there had been any fires nearby."

Joyce set Luna up at one of the library computers. "You'll need to check old newspapers," she said. "I've entered some keywords to get you started. Let me know if you need more help."

Luna grinned. "Thanks, Joyce."

She began combing through the list of search results. There were a few articles about forest fires. One mentioned a house fire, but it had been on the opposite side of the lake.

Finally, a headline caught Luna's eye: "Accidental Fire Destroys Family Home." It was from 25 years ago.

Luna clicked the link. A grainy newspaper article and photo appeared. The photo made Luna raise her eyebrows. It looked just like Boater's painting of the barn on fire.

The story described a fire near the lake. A teen had thrown a party while her parents were out of town. Several kids had set off fireworks. Later that night, the teen awoke to find her family's house and barn on fire. She ran to a neighbor's house for help. But firefighters did not arrive in time to save the property. They thought embers from the fireworks likely started the blaze. It was ruled an accident.

At the end of the article, Luna found what she was looking for. "The property belonged to Harold and Suzy Lasser. There was no loss of life or injury to humans, but the fire did claim the lives of the family's horse, Dreamer, and their yellow Lab, Bingo."

"Bingo!" Luna exclaimed.

Another library patron shushed her.

"Sorry," Luna mouthed to the woman.

Then her phone buzzed in her pocket. It was a text from Amber.

"Did you get the cake? Where are you?"

Luna had completely lost track of time. More than an hour had passed since she left the community center. Now she had to hurry.

"On my way!" she texted back to Amber.

CHAPTER 17

LATE TO THE PARTY

When Luna got to the bakery, she approached the counter. "I'm here to pick up the cake for the community center event," she said quickly.

The man behind the counter looked confused. "Oh," he said. "Someone else already picked it up. They left about ten minutes ago."

Luna thanked him and raced out the door. She knew she was in trouble as she ran back to the center. When she got there, the party had already started. Parents were greeting their kids. Pizzas had arrived. The cake was sitting on a decorated table.

Someone tapped Luna on the shoulder from behind, startling her.

"Where have you been?" Amber asked sternly.

"Amber, I'm really sorry. There was an errand I needed to run. I promise to explain later."

"That's okay." Amber smiled. "I just didn't want you to miss this. It's your party too."

As the girls hugged, Buddy Cross approached them. "Don't cry, girls," he said, feigning sympathy. "I know you're sad you won't see me for a while. Maybe we can hang out this summer." Then he wrinkled his nose and stuck his tongue out.

Luna rolled her eyes.

Amber turned to him. "Oh, did you want a hug too, Buddy?" she said, putting her arms out.

"Ugh, no!" Buddy turned and ran away.

Luna and Amber laughed. As Luna watched Buddy leave, she spotted Markie Lasser. The real estate agent was talking to some other parents.

"Can you believe him?" Amber asked. Luna didn't respond. "What are you staring at?"

"Markie Lasser," Luna said slowly. "Something about her isn't right."

"What do you mean?"

"When I stopped by her office the other day, I overheard her talking to Congressman Firt on the phone. She mentioned a million-dollar resort deal. Markie said she would get it done. Then she called someone else and told them that she couldn't wait to get her money and get out of Ohio."

"Really?" Amber looked shocked. "But she seems so nice."

They kept watching Markie. She was

smiling and laughing. "Does she look like someone who can't wait to leave?" Luna asked.

Amber shook her head. "That doesn't make sense. Why would she want to buy Uncle Boater's house if she plans to leave?"

"Good question," Luna said. "I also found out something else—"

That's when Luna saw her mom walk into the community center.

"Mom!" Luna yelled, running to her.

CHAPTER 18

WARNING HOWL

Luna hadn't realized how much she missed her mom. Her stay at Boater's was the longest she had ever been away from both her parents. She told her mom all about the past week.

After the party, Mrs. Garza drove the girls back to Boater's house. She stayed for dinner. They roasted more hot dogs over the fire pit. There were s'mores for dessert too. Finally, Luna's mom left. She told the girls she would be back on Sunday to pick them up. Realizing that her time at the lake house was almost over made Luna a little sad.

By the time the girls went to bed, it was late.

"Good night, Luna," Amber said as she turned out the light.

"Good night," Luna echoed. For a moment, she lay in the darkness thinking about the day. She hadn't been able to talk to Amber about Markie Lasser while her mom and Boater were around. But now she wanted to fill her in.

"Amber, guess what?" Luna whispered.

There was no reply.

"Amber?" Luna said again, a bit louder this time.

Then she heard the sound of teeth grinding. Luna sighed. "I guess I'll tell you tomorrow."

Luna felt certain now that she knew what had happened to the animals she saw in the forest. They must have been the Lassers' horse and dog that were killed in the fire. Somehow their spirits were trapped in the forest near Boater's house. *Is there any way I can help them move on?* Luna wondered.

Why Markie Lasser wanted to buy Boater's house was less clear to Luna. Markie had said she couldn't wait to leave the state. It didn't make sense.

Luna glanced at the clock. It was after midnight again. But she wasn't sleepy. She sat up in bed. *Maybe a drink of water will help,* she thought. Quietly, Luna crept out of the room. On her way, she grabbed the flashlight.

Luna tiptoed downstairs. In the kitchen, she found a glass and got some water. Then she heard something. It sounded like a dog howling.

"Bingo?" Luna said quietly to herself. A chill went down her spine. Spirits didn't usually scare her. But this howl was alarming.

Luna carefully unlocked the back door and went outside.

Should I go into the woods again? she wondered. *Maybe I can tell Bingo to go home.* She heard the howl again. Boater's warning about the woods came to mind. Luna knew it was not a good idea to go out there alone in the dark. Still, she was so curious. Without thinking, she began walking toward Boater's studio.

Moments later, an odd scent burned Luna's nostrils. *What is that?* She sniffed again. *Gasoline?*

Behind her, there was a splashing sound. The odor of gasoline became stronger. She turned around and shined her flashlight in the direction of the sound.

Someone was standing near the corner of the house. They wore black clothing and held a large gasoline can. Caught in Luna's light, they froze.

CHAPTER 19

TRAPPED

Who's there?" Luna called tentatively.

She watched as the figure placed the gasoline can on the ground. Her light caught the person's fingernails. They were long and painted silver.

"Markie Lasser!" Luna gasped.

Luna had no time to wonder why Markie was there. The woman began running toward her.

"Amber! Boater!" Luna screamed. "Help!"

Luna turned and ran to the art studio. Luckily, Boater had left the door unlocked. After jumping inside, Luna slammed the door shut and locked it. Her heart was racing. She found a chair and jammed it under the doorknob.

"Pity you had to be here for this, Luna!" Markie shouted outside the door. "It's just that this house is standing in the way of everything I want. So it must go!"

Luna realized that the gasoline smell was even stronger now. Markie must have already poured it around the studio. Then Luna smelled smoke. Gray plumes of it streamed in through an open window.

Markie set the studio on fire! Luna realized. She looked around frantically. Climbing out the high windows would be impossible. *Is there another way out?*

"What's going on here?" Boater cried. The sound of his voice in the backyard was a relief to Luna.

"Hello, Boater!" Markie said with dark glee. "Sorry to have to do this. But it only seems fair, right? I lost everything I loved in a fire 25 years ago. Now it's your turn!"

"Markie, what have you done?" Boater was angry. "Amber, call 911!"

"Help!" Luna screamed from inside the studio. "I'm trapped! Help!"

The studio was getting warmer. Smoke filled the air. Luna coughed. Her flashlight scanned the room. Through the haze, she noticed something. There was a small back door. It was on the other side of the studio. She ran for it.

Carefully, Luna felt the door with the back of her hand. It was not hot. The doorknob was cool too. *Good*, she thought. *That means it's safe.* Luna pushed the door open.

The smoke was thick but she did not see flames. Luna ran into the woods. Her eyes stung from the smoke. Breathing was difficult. All she could think of was getting away.

After running for several minutes, Luna couldn't catch her breath. She collapsed on the forest floor. A siren wailed in the distance. Luna's eyelids felt heavy. Then a puff of warm air hit her cheek. There was a whinnying sound. Just before she passed out, Luna saw a horse looking over her.

CHAPTER 20
START FRESH

A warm, wet tongue licked Luna's face. "Bingo?" she whispered, her eyes still closed.

"We found her!" a man shouted. Luna did not recognize his voice. Her eyes snapped open. The man wore a uniform. On a leash beside him was a yellow Lab.

"Luna, can you hear me?" the man said to her now. "I'm a deputy sheriff. This is my dog, Lucky. He helped us find you. Hold tight. Help is on the way. You're going to be okay."

The next few hours were a blur. An ambulance took Luna to the hospital. Her parents met her there. A doctor checked Luna out. They gave her oxygen. Other than some scrapes and bruises, she seemed fine. She had passed out from the smoke. But Luna had gotten far enough from the fire to avoid getting burned.

A nurse told Luna to rest. They wanted to keep her for a few hours.

After the nurse left, Luna looked at her parents. "What about Amber? And Boater?" she asked. "Are they okay?"

"Yes," Mrs. Garza nodded. "You woke them up just in time. They got out. Boater called us as soon as the firefighters and police arrived."

"What about the studio? And the house?"

Mrs. Garza frowned. "The studio was lost," she said. "Firefighters saved the house though."

Luna sighed. "Boater's paintings were in there. I can't believe they're all gone."

At that moment, Amber burst through the door. Her uncle followed.

"Luna!" Amber gave her a big hug. "I'm so glad you're okay!"

"I'm so glad *you're* okay!" Luna grinned.

"We didn't know where you were. Boater thought you were trapped in the studio. When the officer found you, we were so relieved."

"How long was I missing?" Luna had no sense of how much time had passed.

"Less than an hour," Amber said. "But it felt like forever." She hugged Luna again.

Luna looked at Boater. "I'm so sorry about your studio," she said.

Boater gave her a small smile. "Luna, all that matters is that you're safe," he said. "Besides, I had been wanting to start fresh."

"What about Markie?" Luna asked.

"She was arrested," Boater said. "But first she tried to run. Remember those traps I warned you about in the forest? Well, one got her. She let out an awful howl. That's how the sheriff found her."

"Ouch." Luna grimaced. "Do you know why she did it? I found out her house burned down 25 years ago. But why did she say it was your turn next? What did it have to do with you?"

Boater was silent for a moment. Then he swallowed hard. "Markie and I grew up together at the lake," he started. "When we were teens, it became clear she had feelings for me. But I didn't feel the same way. Then she threw a party one night, and I went. I brought some fireworks. My buddies set them off down by the dock."

"That was the party that caused the fire!" Luna said.

Amber looked confused. "Wait, how do you know all this?"

"You know when I went to get the cake?"

Luna said sheepishly. "First, I stopped by the library. And I found an article about the fire. I tried to tell you last night. But you fell asleep."

Boater nodded. "That was the party. The worst part was what happened the next morning. Markie had a horse, Dreamer. That horse meant everything to her. And it was missing after the fire. Her dog, Bingo, was too. She called to ask us to look for them. I checked the woods behind our house. They were there. Both had been badly burned. Neither survived."

"Those were the animals I saw in the woods," Luna said.

Boater went on. "I went to tell Markie how sorry I was. But she was so angry. She blamed me and my friends for bringing fireworks to the party. Soon after, her family moved away. We lost touch. Still, I don't think she ever forgave me."

"But why did she want to buy your house?" Amber asked.

"Oh!" Luna gasped. "The phone call! I heard her talking to Congressman Firt. There was some kind of deal. Firt wants to build a resort. I bet Markie wanted your property so she could sell it to him!"

"I didn't know that," Boater said. "Luna, would you be willing to tell the detectives? I'm sure they'd love to know."

Luna nodded. "Of course." Then she yawned. "But first I need a nap. It has been a long night!"

EPILOGUE

Luna and Amber stared at the painting. The colors were light and airy. There were pinks and whites and pastel blues.

"It looks like a dream," Amber said. "Luna, is that how they looked to you?"

Luna shook her head. "No, they looked real to me. But I think this is more fitting. I asked Boater to paint them like they were free spirits now. Hopefully they are."

Summer was nearly over. Boater was holding an exhibition of his latest works at a local art gallery. One of them was called

Dreamer and Bingo. Boater had dedicated it to Luna and Amber.

"Hi, Uncle Boater!" Amber called. Her uncle walked up to them.

"Thank you both for coming," he said.

"Thanks for inviting us!" Luna said. "I love the way this turned out."

Boater smiled. "I'm so glad. Listen, I'm going to make an announcement soon. Don't go anywhere. I think you'll like it."

Luna and Amber exchanged looks. "Okay," they said in unison.

So much had happened since the night of the fire. Boater had rebuilt his art studio. The police had investigated Markie Lasser and Congressman Firt. They found proof that Firt had told Markie to set the fires. He thought that would drive Boater to sell the land. Then he could build his resort. Both had been charged and were waiting for trial.

In a way, Luna felt bad for Markie. But she couldn't excuse what she had done.

Boater tapped a glass with a spoon. The chatter in the room quieted down.

"Thank you, everyone," he said. "I have exciting news. This summer, my niece and her best friend were part of the City Clean and Green program. It was great to see young people getting involved in the community. So for next summer, I am working with the city to start a new program. The goal is to share the lake with everyone. Part of my property will become an outdoor classroom. Students will come out and learn about the environment and wildlife. And of course, there will be art lessons too! It's going to be great. Please spread the word."

Luna grinned at Amber. They high-fived. "Next summer is going to be awesome!"

Luna Garza

ACCIDENTAL DETECTIVE

THE MYSTERY CONTINUES . . .

Bone Hills
9781680219791

Coal Spell
9781680219920

Dream Land
9781680219944

Found Glory
9781680219784

Hindsight
9781680219760

Main Stage
9781680219777

Scent of Blue
9781680219807